the Queen's favorite Witch

PAPERCUTZ

MORE GREAT GRAPHIC NOVEL SERIES AVAILABLE FROM
PAPERCUTZ™

THE SMURFS #21

BRINA THE CAT #1

CAT & CAT #1

THE SISTERS #1

ATTACK OF THE STUFF

ASTERIX #1

SCHOOL FOR EXTRATERRESTRIAL GIRLS #1

GERONIMO STILTON REPORTER #1

THE MYTHICS #1

GUMBY #1

MELOWY #1

BLUEBEARD

THE RED SHOES

THE LITTLE MERMAID

FUZZY BASEBALL #1

HOTEL TRANSYLVANIA #1

THE LOUD HOUSE #1

MANOSAURS #1

THE ONLY LIVING BOY #5

THE ONLY LIVING GIRL #1

PAPERCUTZ.COM
Also available where ebooks are sold.

the Queen's favorite Witch

#1 "The Wheel of Fortune"

Benjamin Dickson
Writer

Rachael Smith
Artist

PAPERCUTZ
New York

the Queen's favorite Witch

For Our Magical Nieces,
Rosie Dickson
and Karolina Keighren

BENJAMIN DICKSON-Writer, Logo Designer
RACHAEL SMITH-Artist, Colorist, Letterer
DEWI RHYS-JONES- Divine Language Consultant
LILY BILGREY-Production/Design
JEFF WHITMAN-Managing Editor
JIM SALICRUP
Editor-in-Chief

Special thanks to:
JayJay Jackson
Rob Birchall
Yishan Li
James Wills
Paul Gravett
Ceridwen Scott Roberts
Emma Hayes
Dewi Rhys-Jones
Caroline Wajsblum
Delphine Guillemoteau
...and all our family and friends

Hardcover ISBN: 978-1-5458-0721-7
Paperback ISBN: 978-1-5458-0722-4

Printed in China
October 2021

Papercutz books may be purchased for business or promotional use.
For information on bulk purchases please contact Macmillan Corporate and Premium Sales Department at
(800) 221-795 x5442.

Distributed by Macmillan
First printing

PREFACE

Who Was Queen Elizabeth I?

Elizabeth Tudor was one of the most important Queens to ever rule England. She was born on September 7th 1533, the daughter of Henry VIII and his second wife, Anne Boleyn. She had a half-brother (Edward) and a half-sister (Mary) who both ruled England before her, but neither of them had any children of their own, and when Mary died in 1558, Elizabeth inherited the throne. Elizabeth was just 25 years old, and would rule for 44 years.

Elizabeth was extremely clever – she could speak five foreign languages, as well as her native English, and was very good at playing politics. She had to be, because being queen was very dangerous! There were many plots to assassinate her, and to put someone else on the throne instead. Also, a lot of people felt it was wrong for a woman to rule alone – but Elizabeth knew that if she married, her husband would become king and take all the power. Because of this, she never married, and never had children. She became known as "the virgin queen." (The state of Virginia is named after her.)

Even today, Elizabeth is remembered as one of the best rulers England has ever had. Under her rule, England grew stronger and more influential, and there was more freedom of worship than there had been before. She wanted to help the poor live a better life. She set up schools, hospitals, and orphanages, and passed laws that made it easier for them to work and for children to learn a trade. Elizabeth's reign became known as England's "Golden Age." But life was still very hard compared to today! Elizabeth was also the last monarch to rule England and not Scotland. The next monarch would rule both England *and* Scotland as a United Kingdom. But that's another story…

THE TIME OF OUR MASTER APPROACHES. I HAVE FORESEEN IT.

HE WILL CROSS THE GREAT VEIL... AND ALL THE WORLD WILL SUBMIT TO HIS WILL.

WE MUST PREPARE HIS WAY.

ONLY SACRIFICE CAN OPEN THE GATEWAY BETWEEN WORLDS. FOR THE COMING OF OUR MASTER, WE MUST OFFER THE GREATEST POSSIBLE SACRIFICE...

THE LIFE OF A QUEEN.

TO THE SACRED FLAME, I OFFER A LOCK OF HAIR FROM OUR QUARRY. MAY IT QUICKEN HER DOWNFALL.

THE WHEEL OF FORTUNE TURNS.

IT HAS ALREADY BEGUN.

HOW'S IT COMING ALONG, DAISY?

FINE.

IT'LL NEED MORE ESSENCE OF FROG IF YOU WANT THE EFFECTS TO LAST MORE THAN A FEW MINUTES...

I KNOW, MUM! I'M STILL ADDING THINGS!

WELL, I'D BETTER TAKE OVER. I NEED YOU TO DO SOME DELIVERIES.

BUT I WANT TO FINISH THE POTION!

NO ARGUMENTS, DAISY! YOU KNOW *FULL WELL* MR. SNELLING CAN'T DO WITHOUT HIS POX MEDICINE!

BUT--

NOW, DAISY!

STUPID DELIVERIES...

"THE WHEEL OF FORTUNE"

BY BENJAMIN DICKSON AND RACHAEL SMITH

MAKE WAY FOR YOUR QUEEN!

THEY MUST BE GOING BACK TO HAMPTON COURT.

WHO'S THAT ON THE LAST HORSE?

THAT'LL BE THE ROYAL WITCH.

THE QUEEN HAS A ROYAL WITCH...?

SHE NEEDS PROTECTION FROM ILLNESSES AND CURSES TOO. PROBABLY MORE THAN MOST.

SHE LOOKS PRETTY ILL HERSELF...

≷AHEM.≷

EXCUSE ME, YOUNG LADY. DO YOU HAVE A DIVINING CRYSTAL FOR SALE? I SEEM TO HAVE LOST MINE.

SORRY, I DON'T THINK WE SELL THOSE.

ER... WHAT'S THAT IN YOUR BEARD?

MY BEARD...?

GOOD GRIEF! MY CRYSTAL! HOW DID IT GET *THERE*...?

WHAT ARE YOU DOING?

OH, I USE THE CRYSTAL TO HELP ME FIND THINGS I NEED. IT'S MUCH BETTER THAN WRITING A SHOPPING LIST.

DAISY, WHY DON'T YOU SHOW HIM THE GOOD LUCK POTION?

DO YOU WANT TO TRY IT?

HMM! APPARENTLY, I DO!

FUNNY. I'VE NEVER NEEDED A GOOD LUCK POTION BEFORE...

I'LL TAKE IT!

14

HELLO, MEGAN!

HI, JEROME!

DAISY, OUR DOG'S HAD PUPPPIES! YOU'VE GOT TO COME AND SEE!

CAN I GO...?

ALRIGHT.

I'M WORRIED, MEGAN. DAISY'S REALLY BECOMING DIFFICULT. SHE'S STILL SUCH A NAÏVE GIRL... SHE DOESN'T UNDERSTAND WHAT THE WORLD IS REALLY LIKE.

I KNOW. I WISH I COULD'VE KEPT MY JEROME AS THE LITTLE BOY HE USED TO BE. BUT THERE AIN'T ANY SPELLS FOR THAT...AND EVEN IF THERE WERE, HE WOULDN'T THANK ME FOR IT. WE HAVE TO LET THEM GO, SOONER OR LATER. LET 'EM MAKE THEIR OWN MISTAKES.

DAISY'S NOT A FARMER'S SON, MEGAN. SHE WAS BORN A *WITCH!* MISTAKES IN WITCHCRAFT CAN COST YOU YOUR *LIFE*...

"*ROYAL WITCH REQUIRED...*"? WHY ARE YOU SHOWING ME THIS? YOU'RE NOT THINKING OF *APPLYING*, ARE YOU?...

...ARE YOU?

MOTHER, PLEASE...

NOW YOU LISTEN TO ME, *DAISY SPARROW!* HOW MANY PEOPLE DO YOU THINK WOULD APPLY FOR THAT ROLE? HOW MANY WOULD BE THE DAUGHTERS OF LORDS, OR BARONS? SOMEONE THE QUEEN'S COURT ALREADY KNOWS? WE'RE *POOR*, DAISY! WE'RE *NOTHING* TO PEOPLE LIKE THEM!

EVEN IF YOU GOT IT, DO YOU HAVE ANY IDEA HOW DANGEROUS IT WOULD BE?! I WOULD RATHER YOU BECAME A HANGMAN'S APPRENTICE!

19

LOOK AT ME. I'M FOURTEEN YEARS OLD NOW. I'M AN ADULT! BUT WHAT DO I HAVE TO LOOK FORWARD TO? A LIFE OF HERDING SHEEP. AND NO POSSIBILITY OF EVER DOING ANYTHING ELSE.

BUT *YOU...?* YOU'VE GOT A *SKILL!* AND I THINK YOU SHOULD *USE* IT!

BUT MY MUM--

YOU'RE *TWELVE*, DAISY. YOUR MUM CAN'T TELL YOU WHAT TO DO ANYMORE. I THINK YOU SHOULD JUST DO IT! AND IF SHE DOESN'T LIKE IT, *TOO BAD!*

MAYBE YOU'RE RIGHT. OPPORTUNITIES LIKE THIS DON'T COME BY EVERY DAY...

ABSOLUTELY!

BESIDES, IF YOU DON'T AT LEAST *TRY* FOR THE JOB, YOU'LL NEVER KNOW WHAT YOU *COULD'VE BEEN*.

...JUST WHERE DO YOU THINK YOU'RE GOING?!

WHOOMF

YOU'RE GOING TO HAMPTON COURT, AREN'T YOU?!

I WAS GOING TO WRITE YOU A LETTER...

THAT'S *IT!* I'VE *HAD IT* WITH YOU, *DAISY SPARROW!* YOU ARE *NOT* GOING TO THAT *PALACE!*

NOT *NOW!* NOT *EVER!*

IT'S *MY* DECISION! I'M *TWELVE YEARS OLD,* YOU CAN'T TELL ME WHAT TO *DO* ANYMORE! I'M *GOING* TO HAMPTON COURT, AND I'M *GOING* TO BE THE *ROYAL WITCH!*

DO YOU *SERIOUSLY* THINK THE ROYAL COURT WOULD PICK YOU? EVEN LOOK AT YOU?! AND EVEN IF THEY *DID,* YOU'RE *NOT READY* FOR WHAT'S OUT THERE! TRUST ME, I KNOW!

I'VE MADE UP MY MIND.

DAISY...

DAISY, *PLEASE!*

YOU'RE HERE FOR THE AUDITIONS?

YES! I'M DAISY!

WHAT FAMILY ARE YOU FROM?

ER...

WHAT'S YOUR *FAMILY NAME*, GIRL?!

SPARROW...

"SPARROW"? I DON'T THINK I'VE HEARD OF THAT FAMILY. WHAT DO YOU DO?

MY MOTHER SELLS POTIONS. AT THE MARKET...

HMPH.

I'M SORRY, BUT WE HAVE ALL THE APPLICANTS WE NEED FROM *GOOD FAMILIES* ALREADY. THANK YOU.

SLAM

WAIT! I...

...I CAN DO IT...

'ERE, WHY DON'T YOU GO HOME? YOU'LL CATCH YOUR DEATH AT THIS RATE.

I *CAN'T* GO HOME AFTER JUST *ONE NIGHT!* IT WOULD BE-- WELL...I JUST *CAN'T!*

WHAT YOU GONNA DO?

I DON'T KNOW. I DON'T THINK I KNOW ANYONE IN LONDON.

WELL, YOU CAN'T STAY *HERE* ALL NIGHT!

COCK-A-DOODLE-DOOO!

YOU KNOW, I 'EARD THEY WERE LOOKIN' FOR A NEW MAID.

A WH-WH-WHAT?

YOU KNOW, CLEANIN', SWEEPIN', MAKIN' FIRES, ALL THAT. CAN YOU DO THAT SORT O' THING?

Y-Y-YES...

COME ON, THEN. LET'S GET YOU INSIDE.

...I THINK YOU'RE CRAZY, LEAVING A WARM HOME FOR A PLACE LIKE THIS. THIS WORLD IS MORE CUT-THROAT THAN THE SEEDIEST BACK-STREET PUB.

≥SOB!≤

LOOK...YOU'RE HERE NOW. I GUESS I CAN SHARE THE ROOM, IF YOU PROMISE TO KEEP TO YOUR HALF. AND IF YOU DON'T SNORE TOO MUCH...

≥SNIFF!≤ THANK YOU... ER...

NATHANIEL.

...NATHANIEL.

ACHOO!

AH, YOU MUST BE DAISY! I'M EDITH, I'M HERE TO --

ACHOO!

...SHOW YOU THE ROPES.

GIRLS! WELCOME TO HAMPTON COURT. I THINK I SEE A COUPLE OF FAMILIAR FACES AMONG YOU...?

FOR THOSE WHO DON'T KNOW ME, MY NAME IS GLOBBARD, HER MAJESTY'S LORD CHAMBERLAIN. IT'S MY JOB TO FIND A NEW ROYAL WITCH!

OF COURSE, I DON'T HAVE TO TELL YOU HOW IMPORTANT THIS ROLE IS. THE QUEEN HAS MANY ENEMIES, HERE AND ABROAD.

CURSES, POISONS, MALADIES, EVIL SPIRITS... HER MAJESTY IS FACED WITH SUCH ATTACKS ON AN ALMOST DAILY BASIS! IT'LL BE YOUR JOB TO DEFEND HER FROM SUCH THREATS!

ACHOO!

ER. SORRY.

AS I WAS SAYING--

ACHOO!

GIRL, IF YOU CAN'T CONTROL YOUR NOSE, PERHAPS I SHOULD *REMOVE* IT FOR YOU!

I'M SORRY...

DON'T YOU KNOW SERVANTS SHOULD BE *SEEN* AND NOT *HEARD?!* THOUGH, IN YOUR CASE, I'D RATHER NOT *SEE* YOU *EITHER!*

LEAVE HER ALONE, SHE *SAID* SHE WAS SORRY!

HOW *DARE* YOU SPEAK TO ME LIKE THAT!

YOU TWO, OUT! NOW!

COME ON, EDITH, LET'S GO.

I'M SORRY ABOUT THAT, GIRLS. IT'S DIFFICULT TO GET GOOD STAFF, EVEN IN THE PALACE...

NOW, WHERE WERE WE...?

37

WAIT...I REMEMBER YOU! YOU SOLD ME A GOOD LUCK POTION. IT WASN'T BAD. WHAT ARE YOU DOING IN MY STUDY?

I...I WAS MAKING A POTION. TO HELP A FRIEND STOP SNEEZING...

ODD THING FOR A *MAID* TO DO.

I'M NOT REALLY A MAID...WELL, I *AM*, BUT... I MEAN, I'M A WITCH! I WANTED TO BE THE *ROYAL* WITCH, BUT... THEY WON'T LET ME COMPETE.

HMMPH.

YOU SEE THOSE TAROT CARDS ON THE FLOOR? PICK ONE UP AND GIVE IT TO ME.

FASCINATING.

...MOST FASCINATING INDEED...

SNIFF! SNIFF!

HMM. A CURE FOR *SNEEZING*, YOU SAY?

Y...YES.

HOLD STILL A MOMENT...

WHAT ARE YOU DOING...?

...IT *WASN'T* THE POTION...

DO YOU KNOW WHO I AM?

D...DOCTOR DEE?

YES. I'M JOHN DEE. I IMAGINE YOU'VE HEARD SOME INTERESTING RUMORS ABOUT ME?

YES, BUT... YOU DON'T LOOK LIKE A HERETIC TO *ME*...

OH, I AM A HERETIC! MOST ASSUREDLY SO! I'VE MADE IT MY LIFE'S WORK TO TRY AND UNDERSTAND OUR WORLD. HOW IT WORKS, THE WHYS AND WHEREFORES... UNFORTUANTELY, IN THIS DAY AND AGE, ONE CAN'T DO SUCH A THING *WITHOUT* COMMITTING HERESY.

AND IF THERE'S ONE THING I'VE LEARNED SO FAR...IT'S THAT DESTINY IS A FUNNY THING...DO YOU STILL WANT TO BE THE ROYAL WITCH?

OH, *YES!*

VERY WELL. YOU'LL ATTEND YOUR FIRST TRIAL TOMORROW.

...I'M GLAD TO SEE YOU ALL PERFORMING SO WELL. BUT I'M AFRAID THE TRIALS WILL GET MUCH HARDER FROM NOW ON.

YES, WHAT IS IT, GIRL?

WHAT...?

≥HMMPH.≤ IT SEEMS WE HAVE AN EXTRA CONTENDER. *DAISY*, IS IT...?

YES, SIR...

WELL...GO AND STAND WITH THE OTHERS.

ISN'T SHE ONE OF THE *MAIDS*...?

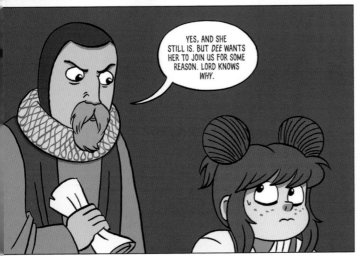

YES, AND SHE STILL IS. BUT *DEE* WANTS HER TO JOIN US FOR SOME REASON. LORD KNOWS *WHY*.

AS LONG AS SHE DOESN'T FORGET HER *PLACE*...

TODAY'S TEST WILL INVOLVE SETTING A TASK FOR YOUR FAMILIARS. I TRUST YOU ALL BROUGHT YOURS?

...YES?

ER...WHAT'S A *FAMILIAR*?

HAHAHAHA

GIRL, A FAMILIAR IS A WITCH'S ANIMAL COMPANION! YOU DO *HAVE* A FAMILIAR, DON'T YOU...?

ER... NO...

OH, DEAR...WELL WHY DON'T YOU MAKE YOURSELF USEFUL AND LIGHT THE CAULDRONS? THE OTHER GIRLS HAVE ALREADY COMPLETED THAT TASK. YOU *CAN* DO *THAT*, CAN'T YOU...?

OF COURSE...

NNNGH!

NNNNNGG!

HEH HEH...

...IF YOU CAN'T EVEN LIGHT A *FIRE*, WHAT EXACTLY ARE YOU *DOING* HERE?

I *CAN* LIGHT A FIRE! I...I JUST CAN'T DO IT WHEN YOU'RE ALL *STARING* AT ME!

HAHAAHAHAHA!

WHY DON'T YOU GO BACK TO SCRUBBING THE FLOOR? THAT'S WHERE YOU *BELONG*, ISN'T IT?

HAHAHA! HAHAHAH! HAH!

YOU KNOW ALL THOSE GIRLS HAVE HAD PROFESSIONAL TRAINING, DON'T YOU? FROM WHAT YOU'VE TOLD ME, YOU'VE JUST HAD YOUR MUM TO TEACH YOU. I MEAN, NO OFFENSE TO YOUR MUM OR ANYTHING. BUT MAYBE WHAT YOU NEED IS SOME PROPER TRAINING.

BUT WHAT USE IS IT...? WHERE AM I GOING TO FIND A FAMILIAR?

WELL, I HATE TO POINT OUT THE OBVIOUS...BUT HAS IT OCCURRED TO YOU THAT YOU'RE SHARING YOUR ROOM WITH A *TALKING RAT*?

YOU... YOU'D BE MY FAMILIAR?

SURE, I GUESS. IF YOU PROMISE TO BE A *LITTLE* LESS READY TO THROW IN THE TOWEL NEXT TIME.

RIGHT. IT'S TIME I INTRODUCED YOU TO A FRIEND OF MINE...

FFA ... SBIGOGLYS ... CIG MOCH WEDI'I HALLTU ...

IT'S WORKING! THEY'RE GOING INTO THE BAG!

OI! VALENTYNE!

PPPBBBRRTTT!

NOT NOW!

WERE YOU... TALKING TO THAT RAT...?

GOOD LORD, NO! RATS CAN'T TALK, MY DEAR LADY! TRUST ME, I KNOW THESE THINGS!

WHAT WAS THAT?

JUST WINDING HIM UP. COME ON, WE'LL CATCH HIM AT HOME.

49

...THAT WASN'T FUNNY, NATHANIEL! YOU NEARLY BLEW THE WHOLE JOB!

OH, COME ON, I KNOW YOU GET A KICK OUT OF IT.

HERE, LET ME INTRODUCE YOU TO DAISY. SHE'S IN NEED OF *WITCH TRAINING*.

RAT CATCHER

...DEE?

'FRAID SO.

HMM. YOU'D BETTER COME IN THEN.

...ALRIGHT, LADS! IT'S SAFE!

HORAAY!

YIPPEE!

THEY'RE ALL MY FRIENDS.

VALENTYNE BASICALLY TARGETS A HOUSE, HIS FRIENDS GO IN AND LIVE THERE FOR A FEW DAYS, EAT THEIR FOOD...THEN THE OWNERS PAY FOR VALENTYNE TO TAKE THEM ALL AWAY!

YOU'RE A CON MAN?

WELL, IT'S NOT LIKE I *DON'T* CLEAR THE HOUSE OF RATS...

BUT NEVER MIND ME. WHAT DO YOU NEED?

I... I CAN'T LIGHT A FIRE WHEN PEOPLE ARE WATCHING ME. IT'S LIKE I... I JUST FREEZE UP, AND IT WON'T COME.

AH, *IGNISRETENTION.* IT'S NOT UNCOMMON IN YOUNG WITCHES.

IT'S *SO* EMBARASSING...

WHY DO YOU CARE WHAT OTHER PEOPLE THINK?

WELL... DOESN'T EVERYONE?

I DON'T. DO YOU THINK I COULD DO THIS JOB IF I DID?

ANYWAY, THAT CAN WAIT.

LET'S LOOK AT YOUR FIRE TECHNIQUE.

WHOOMPH

...HMMPH.

ALRIGHT, STAND BY YOUR CAULDRON.

TODAY YOU WILL EACH BE TESTED ON YOUR PROWESS WITH POTIONS. I HAVE HERE A NUMBER OF INDIVIDUALS WITH...UNFORTUNATE AFFLICTIONS. YOUR JOB WILL BE TO HEAL THEM! GOOD LUCK, EVERYONE.

ER...IS IT *SUPPOSED* TO DO THAT?

OF COURSE! IT HELPS PURIFY THE POTION.

AAAAAAH! NO!

...LOOKS LIKE OTHERS ARE STRUGGLING...

NATHANIEL, I'M TRYING TO *CONCENTRATE!*

ONE SPOONFUL SHOULD BE ENOUGH...

BLIMEY, MISS! I'M CURED!

I'LL GIVE YOU A VIAL TO TAKE AWAY. YOU'LL NEED TO TAKE ONE SPOONFUL EACH DAY FOR A COUPLE OF WEEKS TO MAKE SURE IT DOESN'T COME BACK.

HEY, CAN YOU CURE ME AS WELL?

AND ME!

WHAT ARE YOU DOING?! YOU'RE *MY* PATIENT!

BUT HER POTION'S *BETTER!*

YOU UNGRATEFUL PEASANT...!

...I COULDN'T *BELIEVE* IT! YOUR HEALING POWERS ARE *AMAZING!*

THAT WAS VERY IMPRESSIVE WORK. SUCH A TALENTED GIRL DESERVES TO HAVE *FRIENDS.* NOT *US,* OF COURSE. IT WOULDN'T BE PROPER TO BE FRIENDS WITH SOMEONE OF *YOUR* STATURE. SO WE FOUND SOME MORE...*BEFITTING* FRIENDS FOR YOU...

SAY HELLO TO YOUR NEW **FRIENDS,** DAISY!

AAAAAH!

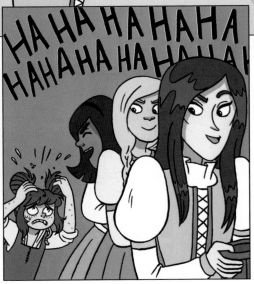

HA HA HA HA HA HA HA HA HA HA HA HA

WOW...SHE REALLY HAS IT IN FOR YOU...

I'D LIKE TO SMASH THAT BUCKET OVER HER HEAD, THE STUCK-UP *COW*...

I WOULDN'T IF *I* WERE YOU. THAT'S *JUDITH HIGHMAN*... SHE'S THE SHERIFF OF LONDON'S *DAUGHTER*.

REALLY...?

HER DAD'S BEEN TRYING TO GET INTO THE QUEEN'S COURT FOR *YEARS*. I GUESS THIS IS HIS LATEST ATTEMPT.

FORGET ABOUT HER. WHAT'S YOUR NEXT *TASK*?

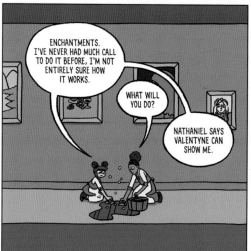

ENCHANTMENTS. I'VE NEVER HAD MUCH CALL TO DO IT BEFORE, I'M NOT ENTIRELY SURE HOW IT WORKS.

WHAT WILL YOU DO?

NATHANIEL SAYS VALENTYNE CAN SHOW ME.

I...NEVER THOUGHT IT WOULD BE THIS *HARD*.

THE COMPETITION?

I DON'T KNOW. ALL OF IT I SUPPOSE. I'M NOT SURE WHAT I'LL DO IF I DON'T WIN. PERHAPS, I'LL BE NOTHING BUT A *MAID* ALL MY LIFE.

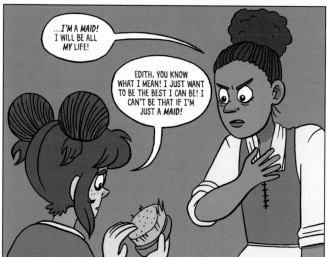

...I'M A *MAID!* I WILL BE ALL *MY LIFE!*

EDITH, YOU KNOW WHAT I MEAN! I JUST WANT TO BE THE BEST I CAN BE! I CAN'T BE THAT IF I'M JUST A *MAID!*

MY SHIFT FINISHED TEN MINUTES AGO. YOU CAN FINISH THE FLOOR YOURSELF.

WAIT! EDITH...!

...THERE ARE *ALWAYS* PLOTS, DEE. WHY SHOULD WE BE SO CONCERNED WITH THIS ONE?

I HAVE NO PROOF, MA'AM... ONLY SUSPICIONS. BUT I BELIEVE IT'S RELATED TO THE POSITION OF ROYAL WITCH.

IF AN ENEMY OF THE CROWN FOUND THEMSELVES IN SUCH A POSITION OF POWER... IT COULD BE VERY SERIOUS INDEED.

AND YOU HAVE NO IDEA WHO THE PERPETRATOR IS?

I FEAR NOT.

ZZZZZZZZZZZZ...

I'M TAKING STEPS TO ROOT THEM OUT.

ZZZZZZZZZ...

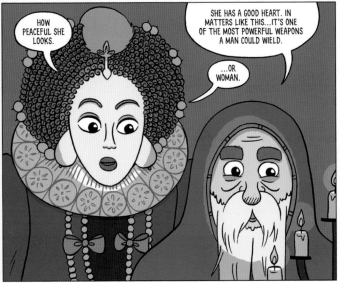

HOW PEACEFUL SHE LOOKS.

SHE HAS A GOOD HEART. IN MATTERS LIKE THIS...IT'S ONE OF THE MOST POWERFUL WEAPONS A MAN COULD WIELD.

...OR WOMAN.

ZZZZZZZZZZ...

INDEED.

I LEAVE THE MATTER IN YOUR CAPABLE HANDS, DEE. KEEP ME INFORMED.

MA'AM.

WHAT DOES VALENTYNE SAY?

THAT WE'RE PLAYING A DANGEROUS GAME.

THAT'S POLITICS.

GENTLY, DAISY.

RAT CATCHER

NNG.

YOU'RE CONCENTRATING TOO HARD. JUST LET IT *FLOW* OUT OF YOU.

WATCH ME.

...YOU MAKE IT LOOK SO *EASY!* WHY CAN'T *I* DO THAT?!

BECAUSE YOU'RE TRYING TO *FORCE* IT.

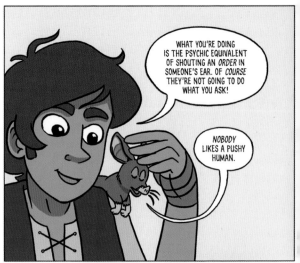

WHAT YOU'RE DOING IS THE PSYCHIC EQUIVALENT OF SHOUTING AN *ORDER* IN SOMEONE'S EAR. OF *COURSE* THEY'RE NOT GOING TO DO WHAT YOU ASK!

NOBODY LIKES A PUSHY HUMAN.

WOULD IT WORK BETTER WITH *NATHANIEL?*

WHAT?!

I WOULDN'T RECOMMEND IT. HE'D PROBABLY NEVER SPEAK TO YOU AGAIN.

THIS IS THE PROBLEM WITH ENCHANTMENTS. THEY'RE SO ANTISOCIAL.

BUT YOU GET *YOUR* RATS TO DO WHATEVER YOU *WANT...*

THEY'RE NOT *MY* RATS, DAISY. I THOUGHT YOU UNDERSTOOD THAT. THESE ARE MY *FRIENDS.*

YOU AND I SHARE A GIFT. WE CAN TALK TO ANIMALS DIRECTLY. SO, IF I WANT THEM TO DO SOMETHING, I JUST ASK POLITELY.

DID *YOU* THINK OF DOING THAT?

VALENTYNE, THE TEST IS *ENCHANTMENTS!* I *HAVE* TO BE ABLE TO DO IT!

YOU *REALLY* THINK AN OLD FOOL LIKE GLOBBARD UNDERSTANDS THE DIFFERENCE?

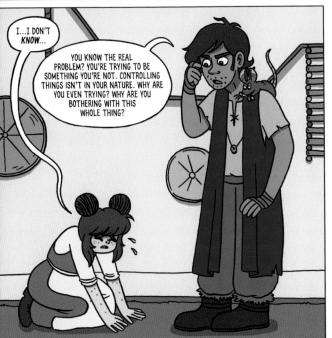

I...I DON'T *KNOW...*

YOU KNOW THE REAL PROBLEM? YOU'RE TRYING TO BE SOMETHING YOU'RE NOT. CONTROLLING THINGS ISN'T IN YOUR NATURE. WHY ARE YOU EVEN TRYING? WHY ARE YOU BOTHERING WITH THIS WHOLE THING?

I JUST...

I JUST WANTED TO BE *MORE* THAN A POTION SELLER...

DON'T YOU THINK YOU'RE MORE THAN THAT ALREADY? IS THIS HOW YOU JUDGE PEOPLE? DO YOU THINK *I'M* JUST A *RAT-CATCHER?*

...WOULD *YOU* DO WHAT I ASKED YOU TO IF I JUST ASKED POLITELY?

I ALREADY *AM*, AREN'T I?

YEAH, BUT... I MEAN, WOULD YOU GET IN A PYRAMID WITH THOSE OTHER RATS?

I'D RATHER NOT. A LOT OF VALENTYNE'S FRIENDS DON'T REALLY THINK ABOUT THEIR PERSONAL HYGIENE.

I'M BEING *SERIOUS*, NATHAN--

OH...

MUM...

THAT'S YOUR MOTHER? YOU SHOULD GO AND SAY HELLO.

...I CAN'T. I STILL HAVE TO *PROVE* MYSELF...

WOW. YOU DIDN'T LISTEN TO A WORD VALENTYNE SAID, DID YOU?

SHE SEEMS TO BE DOING WELL WITHOUT ME. THAT CUSTOMER'S CLOAK LOOKS *EXPENSIVE*.

YES, IT DOES...COME ON, LET'S GO.

RIBBIT.

OH, WELL DONE, JUDITH! VERY WELL DONE INDEED!

THANK YOU, LORD GLOBBARD!

DAISY, YOU'RE NEXT!

YOU MUST ENCHANT...A BOX OF SPIDERS.

HA HA HA!

Dear Jerome,
Thank you for your letter. Things are good here — it's very hard but I'm doing well in the competition. I have a room at the palace which I with a friend.

KNOCK KNOCK

JUDITH...?

HELLO, DAISY. I HOPE I'M NOT DISTURBING YOU. I, ER... I'VE COME TO APOLOGIZE.

I'VE TREATED YOU REALLY BADLY. I... I SUPPOSE I HAVEN'T REALLY BEEN ABLE TO SEE PAST YOUR LOWER-CLASS ROOTS. BUT I CAN SEE NOW... YOU'RE A REALLY TALENTED WITCH.

YOU POURED A BUCKET OF DEAD INSECTS OVER MY HEAD.

ER... YES.

I SUPPOSE I'VE GOT A LOT TO MAKE UP FOR.

...BUT I CAN'T *DO* THIS WITHOUT VALENTYNE! I DON'T REALLY *KNOW* ANYTHING ABOUT SEANCES, AND MY FINAL TEST IS *TOMORROW!*

DAISY, CAN YOU STOP THINKING ABOUT YOURSELF FOR ONE *MINUTE?!* MY FRIEND HAS BEEN *ARRESTED!* THIS IS *SERIOUS!*

...SORRY.

WHAT WILL THEY *DO* TO HIM?

WORST CASE SCENARIO? THEY COULD *HANG* HIM.

HANG HIM...?!

IT MIGHT NOT BE SO SERIOUS. HE MIGHT GET AWAY WITH HAVING HIS HANDS CUT OFF.

BUT...THEY CAN'T...!

YES, THEY *CAN*, DAISY. I NEED TO TALK TO DEE.

DO YOU THINK HE'LL BE ABLE TO HELP?

MAYBE.

PROMISE ME SOMETHING...? IT'S REALLY IMPORTANT.

WHAT?

DON'T DO ANYTHING STUPID BEFORE I GET BACK.

I MAY BE GONE A WHILE.

...I WAS NOT GUILTY OF THE CRIME FOR WHICH I WAS HANGED. BECAUSE I WOULD NOT CONFESS, I RECEIVED NO ABSOLUTION. I CANNOT REST UNTIL MY SOUL IS CLEANSED.

I UNDERSTAND. I WILL ASK THE CHURCH TO GIVE YOU ABSOLUTION, AND TO PREY FOR YOUR SOUL TO ENTER HEAVEN. YOU HAVE MY WORD.

THANK YOU, SWEET GIRL. I'M MOST GRATEFUL.

DAISY! YOU'RE NEXT!

AHEM!

CREADURIAID EIN HUNLLEFAU, GALWAF ARNAT. RWY'N EICH GALW I'N BYD...

CROESWCH Y GORCHUDD, CAMWCH I MEWN I'M TÂN AC Y MDDANGOS GER FY MRON.

76

DID YOU BREAK INTO DR. DEE'S STUDY?

NO...I MEAN... WELL, YES...BUT THAT WAS...

IS THIS FROM YOUR STUDY?

...YES. I'M AFRAID IT IS.

WE'RE LEFT WITH NO CHOICE.

BUT I DIDN'T STEAL IT...!

SILENCE! DON'T YOU REALIZE HOW SERIOUS THIS IS?!

THIS IS THE NECRONOMICON! YOU STOLE AND READ ONE OF THE MOST DANGEROUS BOOKS IN CHRISTENDOM! YOU USED IT TO RAISE A DEMON IN THE COURT OF QUEEN ELIZABETH! WE EXECUTE PEOPLE FOR FAR LESS THAN THIS!

...BUT I DIDN'T KNOW!

I'M SORRY!

LORD GLOBBARD, IF I MAY...I DON'T THINK IT WOULD BENEFIT HER MAJESTY TO HAVE SUCH A SCANDAL MADE PUBLIC. EXECUTIONS ARE RATHER PUBLIC AFFAIRS, AFTER ALL. WOULDN'T IT BE BETTER SIMPLY TO BANISH HER FROM THE COURT...?

HMPH.

AS YOU SEE IT.

DAISY SPARROW, YOU ARE HEREBY *BANNED* FROM HER MAJESTY'S COURT. YOU WILL LEAVE THE PALACE BY SUNDOWN... IF YOU EVER RETURN, YOU WILL BE EXECUTED FOR *TREASON*.

SOB!

WE'LL FINISH THIS UP LATER.

PEASANTS *REALLY* SHOULDN'T GET ABOVE THEIR STATION. IT'S NOT *GOOD* FOR THEM.

WOULD YOU LIKE TO COME WITH ME? I'M SURE WE CAN FIND A PLACE FOR YOU IN MY MOTHER'S HOUSE...

WELL, SOMEONE'S GOT TO KEEP AN EYE ON YOU.

DAISY!

EDITH...

I HEARD THEY'RE THROWING YOU OUT! IS IT TRUE...?

I...I WAS RUDE TO YOU. I IGNORED YOU. I'M SORRY...I SHOULD'VE BEEN A BETTER FRIEND.

HEY, COME ON! DON'T BE LIKE THAT! DO YOU HAVE TO GO NOW...?

I'M AFRAID SO. THANKS FOR ALL YOUR HELP, YOU WERE REALLY KIND.

WHY DON'T YOU AT LEAST STAY AND SEE WHO WON? I CAN SNEAK YOU INTO THE HALL!

I DON'T KNOW... THEY MIGHT DECIDE TO EXECUTE ME AFTER ALL...

GLOBBARD SAID YOU HAD UNTIL THE END OF THE DAY. MIGHT AS WELL USE THE TIME...

MY LORDS, LADIES AND GENTLEMEN! IT'S BEEN A DIFFICULT SELECTION, BUT I'M DELIGHTED TO ANNOUNCE THAT THE APPOINTMENT OF HER MAJESTY'S ROYAL WITCH IS TO BE TAKEN BY...

CLAP CLAP CLAP CLAP CLAP CLAP CLAP CLAP CLAP CLAP

JUDITH HIGHMAN!

AS YOU KNOW, THE POSITION OF ROYAL WITCH IS OF UTMOST IMPORTANCE TO PROTECT THE CROWN FROM ALL HER ENEMIES. NOT ALL THREATS COME IN THE FORM OF ARMIES...

I'VE SEEN ENOUGH. LET'S GO.

ELIZABETH!

BLEUUUUUURGH!

SEE THAT HER MAJESTY IS SAFELY TAKEN TO HER CHAMBERS!

WHAT ARE *YOU* DOING HERE...? YOU'VE BEEN *BANISHED*!

YOU SAID...

...NEVER MIND, I HAVEN'T GOT *TIME* FOR THIS!

JUDITH, THIS IS YOUR FIRST ASSIGNMENT: GET RID OF THAT *GHOST*!

N- NOW...?

OF *COURSE* NOW! WE CAN'T HAVE *GHOSTS* IN THE PALACE, THREATENING THE QUEEN'S RIGHT TO *RULE*!

IT'S NO USE, YOU KNOW! I'M NOT MOVING! I'M *HENRY VIII!* ALIVE OR DEAD, I'M STILL KING!

YOUR MAJESTY.

FINALLY! SOMEONE WHO KNOWS HOW TO TREAT A KING WITH THE *PROPER RESPECT!*

YOUR MAJESTY...I'M AFRAID YOUR SUBJECTS ARE A BIT WORRIED. THEY'VE NEVER HAD A KING COME BACK FROM THE DEAD BEFORE.

WELL...I SUPPOSE IT IS A BIT UNORTHODOX. BUT I'M SURE THEY'LL GET USED TO IT! AFTER ALL, WHY NOT?

WELL...THERE *IS* THE PROBLEM OF YOUR FATHER, *HENRY VII...*

MY FATHER...? WHAT ABOUT HIM?

WELL, HE'S ER... HE'S HERE TOO. AS A GHOST, I MEAN.

HE'S *WHAT?!*

I SAW HIM LAST WEEK. SO SURELY THE RIGHT OF SUCCESSION SHOULD GO TO *HIM?*

BUT...MY *FATHER* CAN'T RULE! HE'S *DEAD!*

WELL, YES...BUT THAT DOESN'T SEEM TO A BE A PROBLEM FOR YOU.

HMM. I SEE YOUR POINT.

YOUR MAJESTY, LET THE LIVING RULE THE LIVING. IT'S ELIZABETH'S TIME NOW. THIS IS HER KINGDOM. LET HER BE.

90

WHAT'S WRONG? NOT JOINING IN THE FUN?

THANKS, BUT I GUESS I'M NOT IN THE MOOD.

OH...?

I CAME TO HAMPTON COURT BECAUSE I WANTED TO PROVE MYSELF. I WANTED TO BE THE QUEEN'S FAVORITE WITCH. BUT I FAILED. NOW I'M NOTHING.

OH, COME NOW! YOU'RE FAR FROM NOTHING. I'VE SEEN YOU IN ACTION... YOU'RE AN EXCELLENT WITCH, NO MATTER WHAT ANYONE ELSE SAYS. PLUS YOU HELPED ME, AND I WON'T EVER FORGET THAT. IF MY DAUGHTER THINKS YOU'RE NOT GOOD ENOUGH TO BE THE ROYAL WITCH, THEN SHE'S A FOOL TO HERSELF.

YOU KNOW, YOU'RE WELCOME TO STAY HERE AS A TOKEN LIVE PERSON. IF YOU WANT.

THANK YOU... BUT I THINK IT'S TIME I WENT HOME.

GOODBYE!

COME BACK ANY TIME!

...I'M STILL ANGRY WITH YOU, DAISY.

YOU'RE GOING TO HAVE TO DO A LOT OF CHORES TO MAKE UP FOR RUNNING AWAY LIKE THAT.

THAT'S OKAY. I DID A LOT OF CLEANING IN HAMPTON COURT.

HMM. MAYBE IT HASN'T BEEN ALL BAD... YOU SEEM TO HAVE MATURED.

DID YOU GET TO MEET THE QUEEN?

YES! IN FACT, I NEARLY KNOCKED HER OVER!

I'LL NEVER UNDERSTAND WHY SHE REJECTED YOU! WHY, IF THE QUEEN WERE HERE I'D GIVE HER A PIECE OF MY MIND...

...AND YOU WOULD BE RIGHT TO DO SO!

...Y-Y-YOUR MAJESTY!

WHY DID YOU NOT RETURN TO HAMPTON COURT AFTER REMOVING MY LATE FATHER?

L-LORD GLOBBARD... HE TOLD ME I'D BE EXECUTED IF I EVER CAME BACK!

HMMPH. WELL IN OUR OPINION, LORD GLOBBARD CHOSE POORLY. WHEN CALLED UPON, HIS CHOICE, JUDITH HIGHMAN, FAILED TO PERFORM HER DUTIES. YOU, ON THE OTHER HAND... PERFORMED *ADMIRABLY*.

WELL... THE THING IS, I DIDN'T REALLY USE *MAGIC*. I JUST...

TALKED TO HIM.

EXACTLY! JUDITH'S FIRST INSTINCT WAS TO FIGHT IT! YOURS WAS TO *REASON* WITH IT. TELL ME... WHICH DO YOU THINK IS MORE USEFUL A SKILL FOR A QUEEN?

I'LL GIVE YOU A HINT. IT'S THE SECOND ONE.

MY LADY, I REQUIRE THE SERVICES OF YOUR DAUGHTER AT COURT. SHE'S PROVEN HERSELF TO BE COURAGEOUS, INTELLIGENT, AND ABOVE ALL, OF GENTLE HEART. ALL THE THINGS I REQUIRE IN A ROYAL WITCH.

WILL YOU ALLOW ME TO TAKE HER WITH ME?

YOUR MAJESTY... FORGIVE ME, BUT...CAN YOU PROMISE ME SHE WOULD BE SAFE?

REGRETTABLY, I CANNOT MAKE THAT PROMISE...I FEAR THAT POLITICS IS NOT A SAFE GAME TO PLAY. I CAN ONLY PROMISE THAT I WILL NOT SEND HER NEEDLESSLY INTO HARM'S WAY.

MOTHER...?

WILL YOU LET ME GO?

DAISY IS OLD ENOUGH TO MAKE HER OWN DECISIONS. IF YOU WANT HER, AND SHE WANTS TO GO...WHO AM I TO SAY NO?

KNOCK KNOCK

COME IN!

AH, DAISY! COME AND GIVE ME A HAND.

HERE, HOLD THESE. HOW ARE YOU SETTLING IN?

MY NEW ROOM IS LOVELY, THANK YOU! VALENTYNE SAYS HE'LL MAKE A LITTLE RUN FOR NATHANIEL, SO HE CAN COME AND GO AS HE LIKES.

WELL, I'M GLAD WE MANAGED TO SORT OUT THAT NONSENSE WITH HIM AND THE SHERIFF.

DID YOU KNOW JUDITH WAS THE SHERIFF'S DAUGHTER?

OH, DAISY, YOU'RE SUCH AN INNOCENT GIRL! I'M AFRAID YOU'VE GOT A LOT TO LEARN ABOUT LIFE AT COURT. THERE ARE FEW SUCH COINCIDENCES HERE.

LIKE THIS...?

...AH. YES.

HENRY VIII

WHY DID YOU...?

WELL, WHAT CAN I SAY? YOU NEEDED...A HELPING HAND.

YOU DID IT...TO HELP ME?

WELL...NOT ENTIRELY. I'M AFRAID THERE'S BEEN RATHER MORE AT STAKE HERE THAN A SIMPLE JOB INTERVIEW.

WHAT DO YOU MEAN?

THERE ARE ALWAYS DARK FORCES PLOTTING AGAINST THE CROWN.

INTELLIGENCE REACHED ME THAT A GROUP OF DARK WITCHES INTENDED TO INFILTRATE THE QUEEN'S INNER CIRCLE. THEY PLANNED TO KILL THE ROYAL WITCH, AND HAVE THEIR OWN AGENT TAKE HER PLACE.

I MUST CONFESS, AFTER THEY SUCCESSFULLY POISONED THE ROYAL WITCH...APPARENTLY WITHOUT RAISING ANY SUSPICION...I DISPAIRED. HOW COULD I TELL WHICH CANDIDATE WAS THEIR AGENT?

THEN, YOU CAME TO ME THAT NIGHT. YOU MADE ME REALIZE THAT I DIDN'T HAVE TO KNOW WHO IT WAS. I ONLY HAD TO KNOW WHO IT WASN'T!

YOU WERE MY WILD CARD, DAISY. I KNEW THAT IF I COULD CARRY YOU THROUGH, YOU'D EXPOSE THE DARK WITCH FOR ME.

THE ONE WHO WAS WILLING TO DO *ANYTHING* TO WIN...EVEN RISK EXPOSING A *DEMON* TO COURT.

SO...JUDITH DIDN'T STEAL THAT BOOK?

NOT EXACTLY. I ARRANGED FOR HER TO FIND IT.

ACTUALLY, I RATHER EXPECTED HER TO USE IT HERSELF. IT WAS A BRILLIANT MOVE OF HERS TO GIVE IT TO *YOU.*

IT NEEDED AN... *EQUALLY* BRILLIANT COUNTER-MOVE.

NATHANIEL... VALENTYNE...YOU ORCHESTRATED *ALL* OF IT!

WELL...I DID MY PART. THE THING WE HAVE TO BE AWARE OF, DAISY, IS THAT THIS IS NOT THE END. THEY WON'T GIVE UP HERE, MARK MY WORDS.

I'VE BROUGHT YOU INTO A VERY DANGEROUS WORLD, AT A VERY DANGEROUS TIME. THIS DARK COVEN IS ONLY ONE THREAT AMONG MANY. MARY OF SCOTS HAS RETURNED TO SCOTLAND. THEY SAY SHE HAS EYES ON ELIZABETH'S CROWN. THE SPANISH ALSO HAVE NO LOVE FOR OUR QUEEN...I FEAR THEY WILL NOT LEAVE US BE FOR LONG.

THE THREATS TO THE REALM ARE LIKE A HYDRA... CUT OFF ONE HEAD, AND TWO MORE EMERGE. WE MUST BE WATCHFUL.

OUR PLAN HAS FAILED!

OUR MASTER IS NOT A FORGIVING GOD. HE WILL NOT LOOK KINDLY ON THOSE WHO FAIL HIM.

WHAT SAY YOU... JUDITH?

I WAS THWARTED BY DEE. BY THE SACRED FLAME, I SWEAR I WILL DESTROY HIM. I WILL BRING HIM DOWN.

BUT I WILL NOT KILL HIM. WHEN OUR MASTER COMES...I WANT DEE TO BE THERE. I WANT HIM TO SEE THAT HE FAILED.

...AND WHAT OF THE NEW ROYAL WITCH?

SHE HUMILIATED ME! BUT SHE'S **NOTHING** WITHOUT DEE AND HIS **LACKEYS.** I WILL KILL HER **MYSELF.**

BE QUIET!

PERSONAL FEELINGS DON'T COME INTO THIS.

YOUR SENSE OF PURPOSE MUST REMAIN PURE. *THE QUEEN MUST DIE,* THAT IS ALL THAT MATTERS. ONLY THEN WILL THE WAY BE PREPARED FOR THE *COMING OF OUR MASTER...*

TO BE CONTINUED...

$\mathcal{B}$enjamin Dickson is a writer, artist and lecturer whose previous works include the critically acclaimed *A New Jerusalem* and the very silly *Santa Claus vs the Nazis*. He has published several short stories in Britain, America, and Germany, and has also collaborated on a number of freely available graphic novels on the subject of climate change. He lives and works in Bristol, UK.

More information at: www.bendickson.co.uk

RACHAEL ♥

$\mathcal{R}$achael Smith is an award-winning comic artist and writer. She has created many critically acclaimed graphic novels including *Quarantine Comix*, *Wired Up Wrong*, *Stand in Your Power*, *Artificial Flowers*, and *The Rabbit*. Rachael has worked on Titan's *Doctor Who* comic series and is currently drawing her new book Isabella & Blodwen.

More information at: www.rachaelsmith.org

WATCH OUT FOR PAPERCUTZ™

Welcome to the graphic novel, THE QUEEN'S FAVORITE WITCH #1 "The Wheel of Fortune" by Benjamin Dickson, writer, and Rachael Smith, artist, from Papercutz, that bewitched coven of commoners dedicated to publishing great graphic novels for all ages. I'm Jim Salicrup, the Editor-in-Chief and Wicked (male) Witch of East Ninth Street, here to talk about queens throughout the graphic novels proudly published by Papercutz.

Let's start with real-life queen, Queen Elizabeth I, shall we? As we discovered in the informative Preface on page 5 she had quite an interesting life. Yet if you've done just a little bit of research on her, such as checking out her Wikipedia page, you've found no mention of there being a Royal Witch among her advisers. So, is the story presented in this graphic novel pure fiction? Perhaps. But then again, what if there really was a Royal Witch? Would that be something that everyone would know about or would it have been kept secret? We'll leave that for you to decide.

© 2021 EDITIONS ALBERT-RENE.

Another real-life queen was Queen Cleopatra who appeared in ASTERIX Volume Two. ASTERIX to those who may not be familiar with this graphic novel series, one of the most popular in the world... well, not all of it. For sundry reasons not worth going into here, ASTERIX isn't as well-known here in the United States as he is almost everywhere else. Ever-optimistic Papercutz hopes to change that and has become the new North American ASTERIX publisher in 2019. This classic comics series, created by René Goscinny, writer, and Albert Uderzo, over sixty years ago, is about a shrewd little warrior with keen intelligence, who gets his superhuman strength from the druid Panoramix's magic potion. Set in the year 50 BC, Asterix's village in Gaul is surrounded by the forces of the Roman Empire. The Romans have taken over all of Gaul except for this one village due to Asterix's and his friend Obelix's superpowered resistance. And if that wasn't enough to infuriate Rome's emperor, Julius Caesar, when he makes a bet with Cleopatra, Asterix, Obelix, and Panoramix are there to help Cleopatra win.

Uh-oh, it looks like I may not have enough room to talk about the queens found in GILLBERT by Art Baltazar and BLUEBEARD by Metaphrog, perhaps we can get to that in THE QUEEN'S FAVORITE WITCH Volume Two? In the meantime, I wanted to mention yet another Papercutz graphic novel that has a potential queen lurking about somewhere in its pages. To say anymore might be a spoiler. Instead, let's have a short preview of this series, about a young woman, Tara Smith, who finds out her life isn't all she thought it was, and eventually finds herself enrolled in the SCHOOL FOR EXTRATERRESTRIAL GIRLS. The series is by Jeremy Whitley, writer, and Jamie Noguchi, artist, and the preview begins on the next page...

We all hope you enjoyed THE QUEEN'S FAVORITE WITCH. In fact, we're hoping you've fallen under this book's spell and will pick up the next volume to see what happens to Daisy next. We'll be waiting for you!

Thanks,

JIM

STAY IN TOUCH!

EMAIL: salicrup@papercutz.com
WEB: papercutz.com
TWITTER: @papercutzgn
INSTAGRAM: @papercutzgn
FACEBOOK: PAPERCUTZGRAPHICNOVELS
REGULAR MAIL: Papercutz, 160 Broadway, Suite 700, East Wing, New York, NY 10038

Go to papercutz.com and sign up for the free Papercutz e-newsletter!

Special Preview of
THE SCHOOL FOR EXTRATERRESTRIAL GIRLS #2
"Girls Take Flight"

MY NAME IS *TARA SMITH* AND I USED TO THINK I HAD A PRETTY NORMAL LIFE.

STRICT PARENTS, NO FRIENDS, NO SOCIAL LIFE.

THEN ONE DAY IN CLASS I SPONTANEOUSLY COMBUSTED.

IT TURNS OUT I WAS AN ALIEN AND THOSE PEOPLE I THOUGHT WERE MY PARENTS WERE ACTUALLY KIDNAPPING TERRORISTS.

I WAS TAKEN TO AN UNDERGROUND LOCATION, SHOWN WHO I REALLY WAS, AND GIVEN A CHOICE.

EITHER I COULD BE DEPORTED OR...

I COULD SPEND TWO YEARS AT THE "SCHOOL FOR EXTRATERRESTRIAL GIRLS" LEARNING ABOUT MYSELF AND THE REST OF THE GALAXY.

IT WASN'T MUCH OF A CHOICE SINCE I'D NEVER LIVED ANYWHERE BUT EARTH.

I HAD KIND OF A ROUGH START WITH MY TWO ROOMMATES.

FIRST, I WAS SUPER AWKWARD WITH *MISAKO.*

THEN I FREAKED OUT WHEN SUMMER SHOWED ME WHAT SHE REALLY LOOKED LIKE, HER TRUE ALIEN FORM.

IT WASN'T MY PROUDEST MOMENT, BUT IT TOOK ME A WHILE TO APOLOGIZE.

SOON, MISAKO AND I WERE BEST FRIENDS.

WE HAD ALMOST ALL OF OUR CLASSES TOGETHER.

WHICH IS WHERE I FOUND OUT THAT MISAKO WAS FROM A RACE OF INTERDIMENSIONAL MAGICAL FAIRIES.

AND WHERE I FOUND OUT THAT MY PEOPLE WERE RESPONSIBLE FOR NEARLY COMPLETELY ANNIHILATING HERS.

WHICH I HID FROM HER UNTIL THE HEADMISTRESS FORCED ME TO REVEAL MY TRUE FORM IN FRONT OF CLASS.

IT DIDN'T GO WELL AND SHE RAN AWAY... LIKE FROM THE WHOLE IMPENETRABLE BUNKER OUR SCHOOL WAS IN.

WHICH IS HOW WE ENDED UP WITH A NEW ROOMMATE, EKATERINA. SHE'S A GIANT CAT ALIEN WHO GREW UP IN RUSSIA AND LOVES AMERICAN MOVIES AND TV.

SHE GOES BY KAT AND SHE AND HER SISTER ZVENISLAVA USUALLY HAVE AN EXEMPTION FROM HAVING TO WEAR THE WRIST WATCHES THAT MAKE US ALL APPEAR HUMAN... RIGHT NOW IS AN EXCEPTION.

ANYWAY, MY EVIL FAKE PARENTS CAUGHT MISAKO AND FORCED HER TO LEAD THEM TO THE SCHOOL... WHERE THEY TRIED TO TAKE ME BACK.

WHICH IS WHEN I DISCOVERED I, FOR SOME REASON, AM A LOT STRONGER THAN THE PEOPLE WHO PRETENDED TO BE MY PARENTS.

PARTIALLY DESTROYING THE SCHOOL IN THE PROCESS.

Enroll at THE SCHOOL FOR EXTRATERRESTRIAL GIRLS #2 "Girls Take Flight"
wherever books are sold!